THE BOTTLE
PARTY

BY

H. C. BAILEY

British Library Cataloguing-in-Publication Data
A catalogue record for this book is available from the
British Library

CONTENTS

H. C. BAILEY

Henry Christopher Bailey was born in London in 1878. In his youth he attended the City of London School, before graduating with a degree in classics from the University of Oxford. Between 1901 and 1946, he worked for the *Daily Telegraph,* first as a drama critic, then as a war correspondent, and finally as an editorialist. During this time, Bailey spent his evenings writing, and became a popular author of detective fiction. He created two series; the first featuring Reggie Fortune, a medicine expert employed by Scotland Yard, and the second featuring Joshua Clunk, a solicitor for lower class criminals. Bailey was prolific, and Fortune featured in no less than twelve collections of short stories between 1920 and 1940. Clunk, meanwhile, appears in eleven novels published between 1930 and 1950, including *The Sullen Sky Mystery* (1935), widely regarded as Bailey's *magnum opus.* Bailey died in Llanfairfechen, North Wales.

THE BOTTLE PARTY

H. C. Bailey

FEW ARE THE cases which have given Mr Fortune so pure a pleasure.

When Carteret Square was built on a swamp, our ancient aristocracy bid against each other for its mansions and put their horses and carriages into a foul mews on the eastern side. The square is now a colossal quadrangle of flats inhabited by the new rich. The stables of the mews have been rebuilt to make garages for some of them and little houses for those who live upon them and renamed, to preserve the dignity of all, Carteret Place.

It is a narrow, prim street, empty, when the children of the chauffeurs dwelling over the garages have been put to bed, unless some knowing creature has left a car parked in one of the bulges provided to give a turning circle for the chariots of the past. But behind the curtains of the neat houses there is often some noise at night, and policemen stroll by from hour to hour.

About eleven on a misty autumn night a constable was pacing along Carteret Place from the southern end when he heard a police whistle blow at the other. He ran upon the sound and, reaching the northern end, found another breathless officer who had heard the whistle, but no one else. They hunted highways and byways in vain. The neighbourhood is prolific in bright young things who delight to take a rise out of the police.

About one o'clock he came down Carteret Place again. The little houses were quieter than usual. But by one of them a man bumped into him and when rebuked knocked his helmet off. They had a scuffle, the man fell, the constable picked him up and dragged him off, wambling in his walk, to the station, and charged him with assault. The man seemed dazed or drunk. With difficulty the inspector got a name out of him, which was Antony Cray, put him in a cell and sent for a doctor.

At nine o'clock next morning Mr Fortune was, as usual, in his bath. Mrs Fortune opened the door and exhorted him to come out. 'Why?' He sank deeper into the water. 'Why are wives?' She turned on the cold shower. 'Not for that, no,' he moaned.

'A lady has called to see you,' she said severely.

'My dear girl! Have a heart. Not before breakfast.'

'Parker says she wouldn't go away. And she's been here nearly an hour. Her name is Valerie Milburn.'

'Not guilty. Means nothing in my young life.'

'You've seen her. She plays the blondes that gentlemen prefer.'

'An actress? Before nine a.m.? Oh no, Joan.'

'I didn't say she could act,' said Mrs Fortune.

The secret of his eminence, he likes to explain, is a capacity to dress quicker than any man, thus making time for higher things. He ate half a cold partridge before he went to his consulting-room and yet half-past nine had not struck when Valerie Milburn sat down in front of him.

The silly, pretty face of the enchantress of light comedy was not at its best. Without make-up her fair complexion looked insipid. She tried her popular, yearning glance, but the smile on the pale lips was a spasm.

'Oh, Mr Fortune, how kind you are!' She used the drawl of allure with which she spoke all her parts, though her voice could put no life into it.

'Not kind, no. Only curious. Who sent you to me, Miss Milburn?'

'Nobody. I came of myself.'

'Oh! Had a bad night?'

She laughed, rather too long. 'There's nothing the matter with me. It's someone else, Tony Cray, Antony Cray, you know, he's the nephew of Lord Frome.'

'I don't. Is he ill?'

'I believe he is, Mr Fortune. It's like this. I live in Carteret Place, you know the dinky little houses there. I had a bottle party last night, starting ten o'clock. Tony – Mr Cray was there on the dot. I'm sure he shouldn't have come at all. You can back him to be on top of the world at any show, but last night nobody could get a rise out of him. He just sat and gloomed. He owned up, about one, he didn't feel too good, he'd go home. Then the ghastly thing happened. Just outside my door a policeman barged into him, the silly brute, got rough with him, said he was drunk and ran him in. They've kept him at the station, they're going to charge him this morning. But he wasn't drunk, Mr Fortune. He couldn't have been. He wouldn't have a spot. He was sickly sober. But you know what the police are. If they get him convicted it'll break him. He hasn't a bean, except what he gets from Lord Frome. The old man was just going to wangle a Foreign Office job for him. That's right off, suppose Tony's in the news for drunk and scragging policemen. You see?'

'I wonder,' said Mr Fortune.

'You could stop it, you could, couldn't you?' she panted. 'He wasn't drunk, he's never violent. Do help him, do save him.'

'The police won't stop for me. Mustn't count on me to save anybody, Miss Milburn. Feeling this rather a lot, aren't you?

However. Curious case. Interestin' case. As you put it. I'll see if they'll let me look it over.'

'Oh, thank you so much,' she started up and ran round the table to clutch his hands.

'Don't do that,' Mr Fortune withdrew them and rang the bell. 'Don't hope too much.' Valerie was shown out gurgling laughter and tears.

Mr Fortune rang up the Chief of the Criminal Investigation Department. 'Fortune speakin', Lomas. Most improperly. To foul the springs of justice. Any objection?'

'I've been pining to catch you at it for years, Reginald. Go on.'

'The woman tempted me. One Valerie Milburn.' He paused for a reply. None came. 'Know her?'

'Not officially,' said Lomas. 'On the stage, yes. The delight of callow youth and aged rips. I thought you had better taste. When did she tempt you? And how? If it's fit for my ears.'

'When? She's only just gone.'

'Good God! Are you talking in your sleep? It's very early for temptation – and for you to be up.'

'I've been up an hour.'

'And fallen for a pretty lady already. Fie!'

'Didn't say fallen. Miss Milburn was woe on the top note. But points did emerge. Her trouble is one Antony Cray. Ever heard of him?'

Again the answer was delayed for some moments. Then Lomas repeated. 'Cray? Do you mean a nephew of old Lord Frome?'

'That's the fellow. Miss Milburn says you've pinched him for drunk and assaulting the constabulary which you didn't ought.' Reggie related precisely all that Valerie had told him. . . .

'Do you believe her, Reginald?'

'What the lady said isn't evidence. However. Statement could be true.'

'Quite,' Lomas admitted. 'Some of these cases are the devil. It's hard measure to ruin a young fellow's career because he had a rough and tumble with the police. And if this fellow was seedy!'

As you say,' Reggie murmured, but he contemplated the telephone with a small, satiric smile. 'Very fair, Lomas. Very human. May I look the case over?'

'By all means,' Lomas said heartily. 'You'd like to see the boy before he's charged?'

'Yes, please. And the police doctor. And the policeman.'

'I agree. I'll send Bell to meet you at the police station.' Lomas rang off.

'Well, well,' Reggie sighed to the dead telephone. ' "Barkis is willin'." '

Ten minutes later he entered the station and met the solid

form of Superintendent Bell. 'This swift attention from the higher powers is gratifyin',' he returned thanks. 'Are you going to tell me things?'

'I don't know any more about the case than you do,' said Bell stolidly. 'But it wants checking up. This way, please.' Reggie was taken to the cell which contained Antony Cray.

He was dirty and tousled and of a yellow pallor, his eyes red rimmed and swollen, his shaking, twitching hands had bled from the knuckles. Yet reason for Valerie's interest in him could be detected. In good condition he might have been a fine fellow, at least a woman's man. He had long legs and a good pair of shoulders, the blurred features of the sickly face were well cut by nature.

'Sorry about this, Mr Cray,' said Reggie. 'I'm a doctor.'

'What do you want?' Cray's voice was hoarse. 'I'm not drunk. I wasn't drunk. The policeman did this,' he held out his damaged hands.

'No drink taken last night?'

'A small whisky at dinner. That's all.'

'Anything besides drink?'

'Yes. I had a splitting headache. I took some phenacetin tablets. They made me all the worse. I couldn't stand the row of the party. When I went out I was dizzy, and stumbled into the policeman, and he said I was drunk and beat me up.'

'Oh. Phenacetin. Often use that?'

'When I get a head.'

Reggie felt his pulse, murmuring: 'Any sickness? No? Rather depressed, what? Did you see things normal last night?'

'With a sick headache? Who does?'

Reggie looked into the swollen eyes and with his fingers on the chin tilted the head back.

Cray jerked it aside. 'Look out! My head's devilish sore.'

'Yes. It would be. That's all, Mr Cray.' Reggie left the cell.

The police doctor, he found, had been told the same tale, and sardonically pronounced it a good story.

'You don't believe it?'

'I never believe 'em. The young rascal wasn't drunk when I saw him, but he smelt of drink. He'd had more than one.'

'That could be, yes. But something else also, what?'

'I dare say. Certainly, I thought him rather down than up.'

'Still is. Not a drunk. No. Nerves all wrong.'

'Well, of course, your opinion is decisive, Mr Fortune,' the doctor was quick to answer. 'If I say neuralgic condition and an overdose of some sedative, that would be about right, I take it?'

'Yes. As near as we can get,' Reggie sighed.

The doctor bustled out.

'Everybody loves me,' Reggie complained to the empty room.

Bell entered. 'The doctor tells me, sir, you and him are agreed Cray was a sick man?'

'Why this kindly joy, Bell?'

'No joy from me one way or the other. I just want things straight.'

'What about the assaulted constable?'

'You want to talk to him, sir? Very good.'

An uncomfortable policeman was brought in. 'This Mr Cray,' Reggie asked, 'How did he collide with you?'

'Sort of staggered into me, sir. But I have to own he wasn't noisy. He caught hold of me, I reproached him. Then he got excited and hit out wild and I had to take him along.'

'Did him proud, didn't you?'

'Sir?' The policeman was aggrieved.

'Bruise under the chin?'

'Then it must have come from his falling down, sir. He did fall heavy. He barked his knuckles proper.'

'Well, well. Nothing more, thanks.'

The constable departed and Bell asked: 'Is that all right, Mr Fortune?'

'My dear Bell. Splendid. Great force, the police force. However. I'd like to see this through.'

'Very good, sir. Come along into court. Cray's case'll be on any minute.'

It went with a rush. The policeman was mild, the doctor masterfully sympathetic. Reggie had just made out the wan face of Valerie watching Cray tell his tale of headache and phenacetin before the magistrate dismissed the charge with soft, paternal words.

'Sort of thing that makes England what she is,' Reggie murmured to Bell as they went out.

'We do know how to be fair,' Bell answered, 'Now would you come along with me? There's a big case turned up.'

Reggie looked up with wide, plaintive eyes. 'Big? What is big? Murder?'

'I want your opinion on that. There's a woman dead.'

'Where?'

'In the Westminster mortuary. Only five minutes' walk.'

'Walk?' Reggie's voice went up. 'My car's here.'

It brought them into the yard of the mortuary. A smaller car stood there, a coupé of class. 'She's inside that,' said Bell.

Reggie gave one glance within and turned. 'Why is she?' he complained.

'I couldn't say, sir.'

'Cautious fellow. Couldn't say whether it was murder! Look again.'

'I leave it to you, Mr Fortune,' Bell recoiled.

The woman's body lay huddled between the seat and the instrument board. Under that her head lolled back, the cheeks, the closed eyes bulged, the nose and lips spread flat. All the face was livid but for purple and yellow marks of bruising. A squirrel coat covered her from bent knees to chin. Reggie drew back its collar. Round the full neck bruises were black to the knot of red bronze hair behind.

He opened the coat wider. Beneath it was a green evening dress. He contemplated that with a pensive gaze which slowly extended to survey the whole of the car's interior before he turned to Bell.

'You don't want to look at her again? Not a cheerin' sight. Not a perfect world. Get your fellows to take her into the mortuary. When she's gone you might bear to look into the car. The higher intelligence could work out a fact or so.'

Bell glowered at him. 'I reckon I'll finish with the car before you're through. If you come back to the station I'll be there.'

Some hours later Reggie entered the bleak room where Bell sat writing, subsided on the only other chair and lit a pipe. 'Not to spoil the story,' he murmured and blew smoke rings. 'Dead woman was forty or so, in good health, well preserved. Married woman as per wedding ring. Cause of death, asphyxia. From throttling with human hands. She died hard. Fought it out.'

'Ah. Clear case of murder,' Bell grunted.

'Oh yes. Not a nice murderer – or murderers. Things

are what they seemed. On that point. Hands were almost clenched. Between the fingers of right hand light yellow hairs, from bobbed or shingled woman. On her teeth some scraps of human skin, colour indeterminate, bitten off assailant. Dress and other clothes not torn, not pulled about, but body and legs heavily bruised. She was on her back and somebody knelt on her to kill her. Murder therefore was not committed in the car. Time of murder indefinitely before midnight. That's the medical evidence. How do you like it?'

'Not so bad, Mr Fortune.'

'Always happy to gratify the higher powers. What is the story you're composin'?'

'I was just putting things together in order.'

'Order is a felt want. Yes. Got it?'

'Well, sir, fairly clearly. That car was found at three-fifteen this morning in Carteret Place.'

'Oh! Where Valerie Milburn gave her bottle party. Where Cray had his scrap with the policeman.'

'That's right. At least in a manner of speaking. The car wasn't at Miss Milburn's house but some way up the street, in a little sort of dead end. The constable who arrested Cray says it wasn't there when he went up Carteret Place at eleven p.m. We can fix the time it was left between eleven and three.'

'As near as that! Better than me.'

'Ah! We might get nearer yet,' said Bell. 'At three another

constable spotted the car. He didn't bother with it, being no obstruction. He came back about five and it was still there. Thinking that queer he looked in and saw the woman.'

'Oh my Bell!' Reggie protested. 'You haven't put things in order. How did it begin? Who is she?'

'Yes, sir. She's been identified. She's Mrs Arundel, a lady living just by where the car was found, and it's her car.'

Reggie blew one smoke ring inside another. 'Who is Mrs Arundel? What is she, that someone strangles her and dumps her in her own car by her own house? Is there a Mr Arundel?'

'Not to my knowledge,' said Bell solemnly, 'but she has had three real husbands.'

'Rather careless with spouses, what?'

'She was no better than she should be, Mr Fortune. A fast woman, half in society, more than half out.'

'The lady's – friends?' Reggie drawled. 'Are they known to the police?'

'She lived in a rackety crowd.'

Reggie smiled. 'Yes, Bell, Carteret Place was having frequent visits from the police at night – eleven, one, three, five. Why?'

'We don't like that street, sir. We have nothing hard, but there is reason to believe it has snow falls. Cocaine, you know.'

'I do. Yes. Though not mentioned when I was introduced to your friend Cray. So Mrs Arundel was suspect of dope dealing?'

'We had her in view. But there have been other reasons for watching Carteret Place, complaints of rowdy parties there and spots of trouble in the neighbourhood. Only last night there was one.' He related the vain pursuit of a police whistle by the eleven o'clock constable.

Reggie sat up. His round face was plaintive and reproachful. 'My Bell! Oh my Bell! Is this puttin' things in order? No. Carteret Place was deprived of the eleven o'clock police inspection. Curious and interestin' fact. Yet I had to pull it out of you with forceps.'

'I'm sorry, sir. It don't signify. The constable went right along the street at eleven and he swears no car was in it. I told you.'

'But he left the street clear. So the car could have been brought along. The woman may have been killed some time before. He didn't come back till one and then he got busy arrestin' Cray. So we don't know whether she and the car were there then. Pity.'

'I grant you there is a look of tricks,' Bell frowned. 'But whistling to get a rise out of the police is a common game with the bright young things round there. I am giving you all the facts, Mr Fortune. When I went over the car I found this–'

He displayed a scrap of pale blue silk. 'It was caught on the edge of the door the driver's side. From a woman's dress and not Mrs Arundel's dress. Hers was green.'

'As you say,' Reggie murmured. 'Not her colour. Dress probably worn by a blonde. Same like the hair in the fingers of the deceased. And Valerie of the bottle party is a blonde. Did you get her to look at Mrs Arundel?'

'Why no, sir. Mrs Arundel was recognised by the constable and then identified by her servant – she kept a house man, no maid, that was her style. I have no reason to think Miss Milburn was a special friend.'

'Till this,' Reggie held up the blue silk. 'Further conversation with Miss Milburn is required.'

'I was going to,' said Bell.

'My dear chap, we do agree beautiful.' Reggie stood up and looked at his watch. 'Help! Have you got a car? Mine has to go home.' He strolled out and, with brief instructions, sent his chauffeur away.

Bell joined him. 'We can walk it as quick as drive, sir.'

'Not me,' Reggie protested, hailing a taxi. But he stopped it at the beginning of Carteret Place. 'Walkin' is only justified when you can't get what is wanted otherwise. As now. In this nasty, neat little street. Where you have to show me things. Mrs Arundel's house. Dead end in which Mrs Arundel's car stood. After that, house of Miss Milburn.'

At that hour of the afternoon, the narrow street was a playground and a mixed club. Children of the chauffeurs who lodged over its garages sported across the roadway, chauffeurs and their wives clustered about the garage doors in gossip.

'That's where the car was found.' Bell glanced at a bulge in the roadway which went up between two houses to a blank wall. 'Used to be a turning circle when this was a mews, often used for parking.'

'Handy,' Reggie murmured, yet out of the way. Good and dark after dark.'

'That's right,' Bell nodded. 'Now the next house but one is Mrs Arundel's.'

It had an emerald green door and russet window frames and curtains of brown netting. 'Suits her complexion,' Reggie murmured. 'By the way, when did she leave the house yesterday?'

'Ah! You're asking something,' Bell grunted. 'Her man servant don't know. He was taking his weekly day off yesterday, and had leave for the night, he says. He went out at two o'clock, went to see his old dad at Kingston and didn't get back till eight this morning.'

'Do you believe him?'

'I have no reason not to. He hasn't been with Mrs Arundel long – only a month – and he's given us a story we can easily check.'

'Will aged father say son was with him at time of murder? Some check! However. Let's try Miss Milburn.'

'There's her house,' Bell pointed. It was some fifty yards from Mrs Arundel's on the same side, a little larger, double fronted, its door, and everything else that could be painted, white. All the windows had boxes of white flowers, geraniums and petunias.

The door was opened by an oldish maid who glared.

'If you please.' Bell stepped into the hall. 'Tell Miss Milburn I want to see her at once.' He held out his card.

'Madam's not at home.' The maid was shrill.

'Do as you're told,' Bell growled, and she slunk away into a room on the right and slammed the door, came out again looking malice sideways and went upstairs. She was not gone long. From the landing she beckoned them.

They were taken into a small room on the first floor, which was entirely white and cream but for two people in it. Valerie shimmered silver grey as she glided to meet them. The man behind her had put his lumpy form into bright blue tweeds and a honey-coloured beard and side whiskers grew on his large pink face.

Valerie was flushed out of insipidity. 'Superintendent Bell?' she smiled and the upward glance of allure had a gleam in it.

'Me too, Miss Milburn,' said Reggie.

'Oh, Mr Fortune. How too kind of you. It was splendid

about poor old Tony.'

'Has he been here?'

'No, did you want him?'

'I wonder. Let's see. About your party last night, Miss Milburn—' Reggie stopped and glanced at the bearded man.

'I was here, sir.' The mans voice was high.

'You don't know each other,' Valerie giggled. 'How futile! On the left Mr Fortune, on the right Ned Patten.'

'Friend of Mr Cray's?' Reggie asked.

'I think so,' the man answered.

'Seen him since?'

'Since the party? No.'

'Mr Fortune! 'Valerie cried. 'Has something happened to Tony?'

'What could happen? Charge dismissed. Revertin' to the party—' Valerie was staring at the stolid menace of Bell. 'Please—' Reggie waved her to a chair and sat down beside her. 'You told me it began at ten. When did Cray arrive?'

'With the first bunch,' Patten answered. 'So did I.'

'Many bunches? Lot of people?'

'Quite a crush,' said Patten.

'All in here?' Reggie looked round the little room.

'Heavens no,' Valerie giggled. 'The state apartments are beneath.'

'Oh! Do you mind – like to look at actual scene.'

'Why?' Valerie gasped.

'Want to make sure where Cray was all the time.'

'But – but Tony's out now. You just said so.'

'Yes. He is. However.' Reggie moved to the door.

Valerie sprang up, slid past him downstairs and flung open the doors on either side the hall. Through one was a narrow dining-room of different gold shades, the other opened upon a lounge, with walls, carpet and furniture all white.

'There you are,' she cried. 'Now you know the worst, Mr Fortune. The lily house. Décor by Ned. Spirit by me.' She made him a curtsey, looking up under her eyelashes.

'Charmin' harmony. Yes.' Reggie glanced at the gold room and went into the white lounge. 'Bottle party buzzed about; what? But the main body here. Were you here all the time, Patten?'

'In and out from the gold room. That's where the drinks were.'

And you, Miss Milburn?'

'I was here in the lounge from start to finish.'

'Where was Cray?'

'Down and dumb in the corner over there,' Patten pointed.

'Poor old Tony,' said Valerie. 'He was sick and hating himself for it.'

'Yet he stayed. Stayed from ten till one.'

'I couldn't shift him,' Valerie cried.

'Silly dam' fool,' said Patten. 'I tried to push him off.'

Reggie looked from one to the other. 'Who else was here?'

Valerie broke out laughing. 'Who wasn't? Hordes! Half my crowd.'

'Mrs Arundel among 'em?' Reggie asked.

That froze them both. Patten spoke first. 'Mrs Arundel was here hours.'

'It seemed like years,' said Valerie. 'She didn't go till after Tony's row with the policeman.'

'Oh. She was still here when he'd been arrested? Quite sure?' Reggie's eyes were set on Valerie.

'Absolutely.' Valerie stared back unflinching. 'She ragged us about it.'

Reggie strolled across the room to a settee. Its rough silk cover showed marks at one end as if it had been scraped by something hard. He bent over it, Bell came to look, they exchanged a glance. Valerie met them as they turned and gasped: 'What, what's the matter?'

'When did she go?' Reggie drawled.

'Mrs Arundel? Some time after Tony.'

'About ten past one,' said Patten.

'How?'

'What do you mean?' Patten scowled at him.

'On her own legs?'

'Of course,' Valerie gasped. 'She didn't have a car. Her house is only a few doors off.'

'I've seen it. So you say Mrs Arundel walked out of your house soon after one. Cray bein' then in the hands of the police. Who remained here?'

Valerie and Patten consulted together with their eyes. 'I did,' said Patten.

'Nobody else?'

'Me of course,' Valerie cried. 'Only me.'

'And then?'

'Then I sat some time with Val and went home,' Patten answered.

'Which way?'

Patten was silent for a moment and grew pale before he answered: 'I live up the street.'

'Beyond Mrs Arundel's house. So you passed it. When did you know Mrs Arundel had been killed?'

'My housekeeper told me this morning.'

'Oh yes. Yes. But passin' Mrs Arundel's house last night, didn't you give an eye to her car?'

'I didn't see any car.'

'Of course we didn't,' Valerie giggled. 'We were only seeing ourselves.'

'Oh. You were with him?'

The giggle faded in a languishing smile. 'It is so hard to say good night. Hasn't anyone ever told you that, Mr Fortune? Give them a chance.'

'I have,' Reggie sighed. 'Good night, Miss Milburn.' He went out.

'You'll be required to make a further statement miss, and you, sir,' Bell told them. 'I warn you what you have said will be tested.'

Reggie had shut the door behind him, and when Bell emerged came from the inner recesses of the hall. 'This bein' thus,' he murmured. 'Passed to you.'

Bell did not answer till they were in the street. 'A pretty couple!'

'As you say.' Reggie stopped and contemplated the house.

'That minx with her goo-goo eyes!'

'Cloyin' damsel. Yes. Cloyin' house. All overdone.' Reggie made a weary gesture. 'Even the side door white.'

'Ah, overdone is right,' Bell chuckled. 'Such silly lying, they didn't know where to stop.'

Reggie looked up at him with pensive wonder. 'That is so. We do agree, Bell.'

'Ah! You got 'em over the car. They knew all about it.'

'One or both. Yes. Lies not so good on that. Smash the rest and all is gas and gaiters. Check the beastly bottle party.' Reggie hailed a taxi and drove off in it.

That night the Chief of the Criminal Investigation Department found him solitary at supper in one of their sprightlier clubs. A bottle of champagne was on his table, he was eating marrow bones.

'Reginald!' Lomas rebuked him. 'And you a married man! Is this domestic virtue?'

'No. Debauch. To preserve sanity. Sufferin' from a public dinner. Mass production food and speeches. On top of your distressful case. The mind was hysterical.'

Lomas sat down with him and ordered a devilled sole and brandy and soda.

Reggie sipped his champagne. 'You may be right. Both equally coarse. Only a wine in name. What's your trouble?'

'Nothing but fatigue. We've done very well. We roped in some of the bottle party and got out of 'em it was an uncomfortable show. Valerie and Mrs Arundel on the edge of a flare up all the time. They've always been cats to each other, but last night well above themselves. They've had Cray in common for a boy friend and he funked both women hard. Mrs Arundel fed the party brimstone scandal about Valerie and Patten. When Cray left he looked dead to the world. On his scrap with the policeman the party broke up. The last of Mrs Arundel comes from a fellow who heard her ragging Valerie and Valerie scolding back. Not too clean, he says. So there's the motive. Then we have the damage to the settee. If the woman was thrown down and strangled there, her heels would have made marks like that.'

'As you say,' Reggie sighed. 'Strikin' and suggestive, the double scrape. Any more evidence?'

'That hair in Mrs Arundel's fingers matches Valerie's. The scrap of pale blue silk in the car was torn from the dress Valerie wore last night. We found finger-prints on the door and window of the car and they're Patten's.'

'Careless animal. Futile liar. So you've taken his prints and searched her lily house. Charged 'em?'

'Not yet,' Lomas smiled. 'We got their prints on statements we handed them to sign. They are detained for enquiries. They'll be charged tomorrow.'

Reggie drank up his champagne. 'End of a perfect day,' he murmured. 'Began by gettin' one rackety fool off a twopenny crime, went on to lag two lying fools for murder. In sweet agreement with the higher intelligence.' He gazed at Lomas with heavy eyes. 'Pleasant dreams. Do you dream? I never could.' He wandered out.

Before eleven next morning Lomas heard his voice again. It came over the telephone. 'I want Bell,' it said. 'Bell in a fast car. With another hefty man or so. At the Oval tube station. Now.'

'Good Gad!' Lomas exclaimed. 'What—'

'I said now,' said Reggie, and rang off.

But when the car stopped by the Oval station, he was not there. Bell fumed for some minutes before a taxi crossed all the traffic lanes and Reggie sprang from it, ran to the police car, slammed the door which Bell opened and thrust himself between the driver and the other man in front. 'Camberwell Road. Let her out.' Between buses and trams the driver did wonders, but Reggie fidgeted and lifted up his voice. 'I asked for a fast car.' The driver flushed and scared all traffic over three busy miles.

Then he was directed into a glum, suburban avenue. 'Slow. Stop,' Reggie ordered. Bell frowned at rows of small houses, each asserting that it was different from the other but of a blinding uniformity.

A man loitering by the corner of a side street turned to look and went on looking.

'Come along, Bell,' Reggie jumped out.

Bell caught him up before he reached the corner, and received a wink from the man standing there. 'My oath!' he muttered, for he knew the man as Reggie's chauffeur. 'What's the idea, Mr Fortune?'

'All present and correct,' said the chauffeur out of the corner of his mouth.

'To see Killarney,' said Reggie. 'Leave your men here.' He turned down the side street.

The houses there were of still bleaker gentility and detached. Scrawny hedges of privet, laurel and aucuba protected each from neighbours and the vulgar world.

Killarney had its name in gold on a red gate. Inside that a monkey puzzler rose over straggling rhododendrons through which a curving path led to the lurid stained glass of the front door. Some noise came out of the house, petulant voices talking together. On a sudden both fell to silence. Reggie took Bell's arm and drew him from the door to a window beyond.

They looked in round aspidistras, upon a dowdy drawing-room and a woman and a man standing close together. Reggie pushed up the window. 'Thanks very much, Cray,' he laughed.

Cray shrank and sagged and stumbled away from the woman. She stood fast. Her purple dress suited the maroon drawing-room, came near matching the mottled flush of her cheeks, but made a cruel discord with the bronze red hair above. She looked from Cray to Reggie and Bell, and they saw her eyes gleam dark.

'Good morning, Mrs Arundel,' Reggie cried, 'this is a pleasure.'

Bell thrust head and shoulders through the window. She

clutched the table beside her, a table on which lay some woollen knitting. She looked again at Cray, who was white and dumb.

'Yes, kind of Cray to bring us along,' said Reggie. 'Superintendent Bell did want you.'

She picked up the knitting, she turned and flung herself at Cray and drove the needles into his face, into his throat.

Bell shouted; Bell clambered into the room. Cray had fallen and she was upon him, stabbing at him with the bestial strength of frenzy.

Bell dragged her off. She kicked and bit, till his men came through the window and mastered her. Reggie was kneeling by Cray. 'Don't be rough,' he said over his shoulder. Handcuffs were put on her, her legs were tied.

'She has done you proud,' he said to Cray, whose throat was welling blood. 'However.' He rose and came to Mrs Arundel. 'Allow me.' He drew her long sleeves back from the handcuffs. On the right arm the skin had been torn and dents showed red. 'Oh yes. Where sister bit you,' he murmured, and the woman shrieked. 'Take her away. Me for the other victim.'

That afternoon he came into Lomas's room dreamy and benign. 'One of your larger cigars is indicated.' He helped himself and sank down in the easiest chair. 'Pleasin' case.'

Lomas took up his telephone. 'Come along, Bell. Mr Fortune's here at last.'

'My dear old thing!' Reggie protested. 'Only paused for a simple lunch.'

'Till half-past three,' Lomas rebuked him.

Bell strode in. 'What about Cray, Mr Fortune? Is he going to come through?'

'He thinks not. I didn't tell him he was wrong.'

'My oath!' Bell muttered.

'Had a confession from him?'

'Yes, sir. Him believing he wouldn't live.'

'Last dying speech,' Reggie smiled. 'Anything like the truth?'

'It's a queer story. He says Mrs Arundel was in the dope business, and broke him down teaching him to take snow. She told him the dead woman was her sister and lived on her, passed her the dope and blackmailed her over it. The trade was bad lately. Money ran short and this sister turned nasty, threatened she'd give the whole game away. She came to Mrs Arundel's house day before yesterday. Mrs Arundel 'phoned him, and when he got there the woman was dead. Mrs Arundel said she'd had to kill her, the only way to stop her mouth; she was going to split on 'em both, but it would be all right if he helped get the body taken for Mrs Arundel's, she'd go off and pass as her sister. But he wouldn't stand for it; he wouldn't do a thing, and he quit. Then this morning he had a telegram:

'Come Killarney,' and he didn't dare not go for fear of her.'

'Fearful fellow. Yes. That's why he's such a brute. He helped to strangle the sister. Hence the bruise under his chin. Any confession from Mrs Arundel?'

'Not a word.'

'There will be. When she hears his. However. Don't matter. Been over Mrs Arundel's house yet?'

'We have, sir. What are you thinking of?'

'Oh my Bell. Settee, divan or bed. Scratches thereon, same like the white settee of Valerie.'

'That's pretty good.' Bell smiled grimly. 'We didn't find anything scratched. But Mrs Arundel's house man says there's an old Persian rug gone from the couch in the drawing-room.'

'Splendid,' Reggie purred. 'Pleasin case. Subtle female, Mrs Arundel. All clear.'

'Clear!' Lomas exclaimed. 'You flatter yourself, Reginald.'

'Not myself. No.' Reggie sank down in his chair. 'Do I flatter you? Surely not.'

'We can convict these two beauties now, but we don't know how the thing was worked.'

'Oh my Lomas. Think again. Believe the evidence. Cray and the Arundel strangled Mrs Jones and she left her mark on both of 'em, some time before ten. I told you she died earlier than midnight. Cray went off to Valerie's party at ten, The Arundel stripped dead sister and put on the body

31

clothes of her own, evenin' dress matchin' the one she wore herself at the bottle party. Not a nice job. Not a nice woman. Twisted some of Valerie's hair in the dead fingers. Next event. Eleven o'clock constable called out of Carteret Place by a police whistle. No doubt Mrs Arundel blew that from her car. Him being gone, Cray slunk out of Valerie's lily house – I showed you the side door, Bell, it opens on a passage where the cloak room is. The Arundel brought her car round, Cray helped her put the body in the car, covered it with the missin' rug, so it wouldn't show and came back to party via side door and cloak room. The Arundel then arrived by the front door. Either of 'em could easily get a bit torn off Valerie's blue dress to shove in the car, easily scratch the settee like the heels of the woman scratched the rug when they murdered her. When the one o'clock constable was due Cray barged out and got himself arrested, thus fakin' a perfect alibi for the murder of Mrs Arundel, then alive. After puttin' up a row with Valerie to make more evidence against her, the Arundel went off, dressed herself in dead sister's clothes, removed the rug from the body, proceeded to Killarney and became the sister. She is just like sister – to those who haven't had close ups of both. Cray was sweetly confident Valerie would swear he'd never left the party and Patten would back her through hell. Kindly nature, Cray's. Perfect trust in his friends. Patten took his good night walk with Valerie. They saw the car, knew it was Mrs Arundel's. They looked inside, Patten leavin' his fool prints on the door, and saw a dead woman. I should say he didn't recognise her. Not easy to see in the dark, not nice to investigate that face. They wouldn't think of it being Mrs Arundel as she'd only just left 'em. But there was a very dead woman in her car. Cray had behaved queer at the party, funking Valerie, lurking. They knew he might have slunk out and done the kill. They hated Mrs Arundel, they liked him, they knew she had him on a string. All they cared for was to save him. They left the woman for somebody else to find, and fixed up they'd give Cray his alibi, and Valerie came round bright and early to rub it in on me he was a poor, sick fellow under her eye all the time till arrested. Dear fools, Valerie and her Ned. Made for each other. Must have hit 'em cruel hard when they heard the dead woman was Mrs Arundel. And yet they stuck to their story. Very good effort. Bless 'em. Nice people. Hope you haven't charged 'em, Lomas?' Reggie smiled.

'We have not,' said Lomas with dignity. 'They were let go this morning.'

'Splendid. Not a blot on the official scutcheon. Now. I have my uses, Lomas.'

'Confound your impudence.' Lomas made a grimace. 'How did you know the Arundel woman had a sister?'

'By believin' evidence. Try sometime. I told you the dead woman was in good health, well preserved. Too good, too well for a woman who'd led a nasty life, as alleged of the Arundel.

33

She shows wear and tear. Dead face so distorted, identification could only be from general likeness, hair, clothes and what not, and the identification was not made by intimates. So I wondered. I sent my chauffeur, Sam, to browse among the children of Carteret Place. Observant animals girl children. They told him Mrs Arundel wasn't always smart, quite shabby when she went on the buses. Some of 'em spotted her the day before descendin' from a Lewisham bus. Not the first time. Sam tried the Lewisham bus conductors, and heard of a lady like the Arundel who got on in those parts and got off at the stop by Carteret Square. Then the local milkman and postman gave him the glad news she was Mrs Jones, of Killarney. Quite the lady, kept herself to herself, most respectable, though only using a charwoman two days a week. Sam called as a tout and looked her over. Me too, from the adjacent aucubas. On which I 'phoned for the higher powers. There you are. All clear, as I said.'

'Is it?' Lomas put up his eyeglass. 'Why did Gray go to her?'

'My dear old thing!' Reggie stared back with large reproachful eyes. 'Use the evidence. Cray told you in his confession. He got a telegram: "Come Killarney." The Arundel had the wind up. Probably failed to like Sam's face. He will grin.'

'Failed to like Cray when he came,' Lomas answered. 'That's what broke her.'

'It could be,' Reggie murmured. 'Don't suppose he was comfortin'.'

'Who sent the telegram?' Lomas demanded.

'Oh my Lomas! Futile question. Answer obvious. Mrs Arundel.'

'She'll deny it.'

Over Reggie's face came a pensive smile. 'She may, yes. Nobody'll believe her.'

'Why should she telegraph? She was on the telephone.'

'Yet she couldn't get Cray? Nor Cray her? Only wrong numbers. Too bad.'

'The line's broken on the wall of the house, Reginald. Who did that?'

'Take the goods the gods provide. Telegram's all right. Pleasin case.'

www.ingramcontent.com/pod-product-compliance
Lightning Source LLC
Chambersburg PA
CBHW030531260626
47157CB00005B/1979